Sheltered By The Sergeant Major

The Brotherhood, Volume 2

Mia Caldwell and Mylia Ashton

Published by Mia Caldwell, 2024.

© 2023 Mia Caldwell

All Rights Reserved. This book or any portion thereof may not be reproduced or used in any manner whatsoever without the express permission of the publisher except for the use of brief quotations in a book review.

This book is a work of fiction. Any resemblance to persons, living or dead, or places, events or locations is purely coincidental. The characters are all productions of the author's imagination.

Please note that this work is intended only for adults over the age of 18 and all characters represented as 18 or over.

Colors of Love Press and the author reserve all rights to this title. Any places, people, or events that resemble something real are coincidental and a product of the author's imagination. No part of this work may be copied or shared without written permission of the publisher and/or author.

© Mylia Ashton, 2023

Blurb

ALMOST FIVE YEARS AGO, Cooper ended things with Nina, convinced he couldn't be a good boyfriend and a good soldier. A few months later, he lost almost everything to an IED. Only his team remains part of his life, until the fateful day Nina drives onto his ranch, with a little boy in tow—his son. Nina's boss is after her, desperate to keep her quiet about his money laundering operation, and she has nowhere to turn.

Cooper swears to keep her safe. He knows how to be a soldier in spite of his crippling injuries. He doesn't yet know how to be a father or the partner Nina needs, but he's going to have a crash course in being a family man. The more time he spends with Nina and Caleb, the more he realizes this is a second chance at happiness and redemption, but only if he and the Brotherhood can keep them safe.

This is a second-chance reunion BWWM with a secret baby, a touch of steam, and a dash of action.

Chapter 1

THE BLISTERING TEXAS sun beat down on Cooper as he finished his patrol of the perimeter fence. The lonely windswept ranch was usually silent, save for the occasional barking of his dogs, Scooter and Lex. He preferred the isolation, having withdrawn from the world after the IED explosion that ravaged his body and his mind. The war was thousands of miles away, but he still felt its effects every day.

As he approached the house, Scooter's frantic barking broke the quiet. He stopped, instantly alert, his hand going to the Glock on his hip out of years of habit. Lex stood at attention beside Scooter, his big head swiveling from the terrier to the driveway. Cooper followed the mastiff's gaze to see a dusty sedan pulling up the long dirt driveway, trailing a cloud of dust in its wake.

Cooper stepped into the shadows, assessing the unfamiliar vehicle with a tactical eye. No one came out here unannounced. His closest neighbor was ten miles away, the nearest town thirty. This car shouldn't be here.

The driver cut the engine but made no move to exit the vehicle, as if working up the courage or waiting for something. Cooper rested his hand on his holstered pistol and moved silently onto the porch. He had no patience for uninvited guests. Scooter and Lex flanked him, their presence comforting. He fixed his sternest glare on the sedan, honed from years of issuing commands on the battlefield. The intruder would either explain themselves or be swiftly removed from his land.

The standoff stretched on, the only sounds the faint squeaking of the car's suspension and the restless padding of the dogs at his side. Finally, the back door opened, and a small figure stepped out.

Cooper froze, momentarily confused. It was a child—a boy of about four years old, skinny and fine-boned, with a mop of unruly dark curls. The boy blinked at the harsh sunlight, peering around uncertainly. After a moment, the driver's door opened, and a woman stepped out. She was older than Cooper expected—late-twenties, perhaps—wearing faded jeans and a wrinkled t-shirt with a wilted air, as if she hadn't slept in some time. Her brown curls were pulled into a messy ponytail, loose strands clinging to the sweat on her neck. Her skin was almost ashen, though he'd bet it was normally radiant brown with a golden undertone when she wasn't so exhausted.

The woman looked over at Cooper warily, then reached back into the car to retrieve a plastic grocery bag. The boy clung to the woman's leg, half-hidden behind her thigh as he stared back at Cooper with dark eyes that seemed familiar, though he knew they had never met.

Suspicion flared in Cooper's chest. The boy's age nagged at him, stirring long-buried memories of a whirlwind romance right before his last deployment, a love affair that had turned to ashes in his absence. It couldn't be. He shoved the thought away. It was impossible.

The woman—Nina, he recalled now—approached slowly, one hand holding the boy's, the other clutching her bag to her chest like a shield. Her dark brown eyes held the haunted look of someone who hadn't rested in days. Cooper straightened, squaring his shoulders. If Nina was here, something was wrong, but whatever trouble she brought to his doorstep, he aimed to handle it swiftly. No one disturbed his solitude on this ranch, no matter their history.

Drawing up before the porch steps, she hesitated, chewing her lip. The gesture sparked a memory—her smiling up at him before he had left on deployment, the last time he had seen her carefree and innocent. Before the world irrevocably changed for both of them.

He crossed his arms over his chest, waiting. He owed her nothing now, years too late for explanations.

Nina released a shuddering breath. "Hello, Cooper. I...I'm sorry to show up like this, but I need help. Desperately." Her fingers worked nervously at the plastic bag as she spoke. "May we come in?"

Cooper held silent. Once he would have moved Heaven and Earth for this woman. Now she was a stranger, arriving unannounced with a child in tow, upending the solitude he had sacrificed so much to obtain. His answers waited behind those walls, best given in private.

Finally, he grunted assent. Her shoulders slumped in relief as she took the boy's hand and ascended the steps. The boy—Cooper still refused to dwell on his unspoken suspicions about the child—flinched as they drew near, pressing himself to Nina's leg as he eyed his scars. Cooper was used to such reactions. Children always shied from his ravaged face.

Inside, Nina perched uneasily on the couch while the boy clung to her, his face half-hidden against her side. The plastic bag sat on the coffee table between them. Nina wet her lips.

"I'm so sorry to barge in like this," she began uncertainly.

Cooper said nothing. Her reasons for being here remained a mystery, one he aimed to unravel soon. His continued silence would encourage her to explain herself faster.

Nina cleared her throat. "I...I tried to contact you in Germany after the explosion but they said you were still in a coma." Her voice dropped. "I should have tried harder once you were stateside but everything was so crazy and overwhelming."

Germany. The word ignited memories of agony and despair in those military hospitals after the blast. If Nina had tried to reach him, the efforts never penetrated the haze of trauma and morphine surrounding him then.

At his silence, Nina barreled on nervously, "It's just, well, with everything happening now, I didn't know where else to go."

The boy chose that moment to pull away from Nina's side and slide off the couch. One hand still clinging to hers, he took a hesitant step forward, curiosity drawing him toward the coffee table. Toward the plastic bag.

Nina made a convulsive movement as if to snatch the boy back, but he held up a hand, stopping her. Let this play out. His instincts were buzzing, prodding him toward an impossible truth, but he must be certain.

The boy reached the bag and fingered it hesitantly. Behind the milky plastic, Cooper could see two apples, a loaf of bread, peanut butter, and a small stuffed dog toy. Food. For traveling. Running.

The boy grasped the toy through the plastic, turning it over with interest. It was military, Cooper realized with a start. A facsimile of a German shepherd wearing an armored vest, of the kind used by special forces units. Why would any child have such a specific, niche toy?

Cold certainty gripped him then, but he needed to hear Nina say the words.

"Why are you here?" he demanded hoarsely. "What trouble brings you to my door after so long?"

Nina flinched at his harsh tone, but finally, haltingly, the words spilled out. "You have a son, Cooper. This...this is Caleb. Your son."

A son.

It was impossible. Unthinkable, but even as denial clamored in Cooper's mind, details locked into place—the timing, the boy's age, the familiar eyes that now lifted to study Cooper's ruined face. Eyes that were a perfect match for his own.

Cooper's pulse roared in his ears. Dimly, he heard Nina's tearful voice recounting the letter gone astray, her desperation that drove her here, but the words barely penetrated the shock reverberating through him.

A son. His son.

With the truth laid bare between them, events took on a nightmarish clarity. They had brought danger to his door—Nina was on the run, and she had dragged an innocent child into the crosshairs, his own flesh and blood.

Protective instinct roared to life in his chest, momentarily overriding the shock and betrayal coursing through him. Whatever Nina's reasons for the years of deception, the boy was blameless. Right now, he needed protecting. Whatever came later, Cooper would ensure no harm came to his son.

Grim purpose filled him as he rose and strode to the gun safe in the corner. He spoke over his shoulder, voice hard and unyielding as steel. "Tell me everything. Now."

There could be no more secrets, and no more lies by omission. If Cooper was to keep his newly discovered child from harm, he needed the full truth of the danger they faced. Only then could he summon the brotherhood and prepare his ranch for the coming storm.

Chapter 2

NINA TOOK A SHAKY BREATH, looking down at her hands clenched tight in her lap. "His name is Darren Silva. I was working as a bookkeeper at his car dealership in Houston." She risked a glance up at Cooper. He was watching her intently, his scarred face unreadable. "At first everything seemed normal, but over time, I started noticing odd discrepancies in the books. Money flowing in and out without clear sources. A lot more cash purchases than normal for high-end cars."

She sighed, shoulders slumping. "It took me too long to realize Darren is laundering money, and now he sees me as a risk."

Cooper straightened, his eyes narrowing. When he spoke, his voice was clipped and direct. "Tell me straight. What has he done, and how much danger are you in?"

"He started with threats to keep me quiet," Nina said. "Warning messages on my car, implied threats against Caleb." She rubbed a hand across her eyes. "Last week, he torched my apartment. He killed my neighbor's chicken and left it on the doorstep with a note warning it would be Caleb next."

She choked back a sob, covering her mouth with one hand. After a moment, she mastered herself and went on. "That's when I knew I had to run. So I packed us up and just started driving. I didn't know where else to go except...here."

Cooper absorbed this silently. Across the room, little Caleb made his stuffed dog dance along the edge of the coffee table, blissfully oblivious to the perilous situation.

Finally, Cooper spoke, his voice low but gravelly with emotion. "You should have come to me sooner."

Nina shook her head helplessly. "I was scared, Cooper. Scared you'd reject Caleb or reject me." Her dark eyes shimmered with tears. "I thought I could handle Darren. I never meant to bring this danger to you."

Cooper ran a hand over his stubbled jaw. "What's done is done. Not your fault that bastard turned violent." He nodded firmly as if deciding something. "But you're here now, and I protect what's mine."

Nina's eyes widened at the word mine, but Cooper was already loading the weapon he'd taken from the gun safe with smooth efficiency.

She shifted anxiously. "What are you going to do?"

He didn't look up from the shotgun. "Call in support. My old unit—we still watch each other's backs, no matter how much time passes."

He finished loading the shotgun and pumped the action, checking the chamber. "They'll be here within twenty-four hours. We'll keep you both secure until then."

Nina opened her mouth to protest, then closed it again. Caleb chose that moment to amble over, his stuffed dog in hand. He looked up at Cooper with a tentative expression. "Are the bad men coming here?" His high voice was worried.

Cooper's stern expression gentled. He crouched down so his eyes were level with Caleb's. "Not if I can help it. I'm going to do everything I can to keep you and your mama safe. I promise."

Caleb considered this, then nodded solemnly. Some of the worry lifted from his small face. He held out the stuffed dog to Cooper. "This is Rex. He protects me from the bad men too. You can borrow him."

Emotion flashed across Cooper's scarred face. Carefully he accepted the toy dog, tucking it into his shirt pocket. "Thank you, Caleb. Rex and I will stand guard together."

Caleb grinned, showing a missing front tooth. Nina watched the exchange, blinking back moisture. Cooper smoothed a big hand over Caleb's unruly curls before standing back up.

"I need to make those calls. Get settled in one of the spare rooms and lock the door. Don't open it unless you hear the password—Rangers Lead the Way. Understand?"

Nina nodded, taking Caleb's hand. Cooper grabbed the shotgun and headed toward the porch, Scooter and Lex on his heels.

After finding the guest room, Nina sank onto the twin bed, the old springs creaking beneath her. She clasped her hands to still their trembling. Her pulse roared in her ears as Cooper's stunned reaction replayed in her mind—that opaque look revealing nothing of his thoughts. She had expected anger, disbelief, and probably rejection, but not the flat emptiness in his eyes.

Across the small room, Caleb sat on the braided rug, oblivious. He crashed two toy cars together, making soft vroom-vroom noises. Nina managed a faint smile. However unknown his father was, her bright boy deserved a chance at safety and happiness. That was all that mattered now.

A knock at the door made her start. She drew a sharp breath. "Who is it?"

"Cooper. Just me." His rough voice was muted through the wood. "Can we talk?"

Nina rose on shaky legs and crossed to open the door. Cooper's imposing figure filled the doorway, but his stern face had softened slightly. Over his shoulder, the front door stood open to the porch beyond.

"Mind if I come in?" His tone was gentle, as if addressing a skittish colt.

She backed up in wordless invitation. He entered cautiously, seeming to shrink the small room. His gaze went immediately to Caleb still playing on the floor. Raw emotion flashed across Cooper's ravaged face. "He's beautiful. Perfect." The words scraped from his throat.

Nina's own throat tightened, eyes welling. Whatever came next, Caleb would finally know his father. That truth gave her strength to face Cooper and discover where they stood after her revelation.

She perched on the edge of the bed. Cooper lowered himself into the single chair by the window, the wood creaking under his muscular frame. He seemed unable to tear his gaze from Caleb. The boy obliviously crashed his cars with youthful abandon, dark curls falling over his forehead.

Nina wet her dry lips. "I'm so sorry," she whispered. "I wanted to tell you. I tried..."

Cooper held up a scarred hand, stopping her. "The past is done," he said. "You're here now. With my son." He shook his head as if still struggling to grasp the truth.

Caleb chose that moment to push up from the rug and bring his cars over to Cooper, gaze curious. "Who are you?"

Cooper's expression gentled. He slid from the chair to crouch before Caleb, putting their eyes level. "I'm your daddy." His voice was thick with restrained emotion.

Caleb considered this new information. "Why haven't I seen you before?"

The innocent question seemed to pierce Cooper's heart. He drew a ragged breath. "I didn't know about you until today, but I'm here now, and I'm going to keep you and your mama safe. I promise."

Caleb mulled this over. Then he held out a blue car to Cooper. "Do you want to play cars with me?"

Cooper's ravaged face softened. He accepted the toy reverently. "I'd like that very much."

Nina observed the tender exchange, eyes blurring with tears. Then Cooper rose and returned to his seat, turning to her with an expression of grim resolve.

"You said this man—Darren—has threatened you?" His tone was all business now.

Nina quickly outlined the escalating intimidation tactics. Cooper's face darkened as she went through it all again, in greater detail now.

"This ends now," he bit out. "I've called in my team. We'll hunt him down."

"No, it's too dangerous—" Nina began.

"It's the only way. Trust me. We were built for this." His tone brooked no argument. He leaned forward, eyes boring into hers. "Understand this. You and Caleb are mine to protect now. No one touches what's mine. No one."

Looking at the iron determination on his ruined face, Nina could only nod silently. Cooper stood up and left the room without explanation. He'd never been entirely extroverted, but he'd at least talked to her in the past. So many things had changed.

Nina released a long breath, gazing at Caleb still happily playing on the floor. Whatever the coming days held, the boy would have a chance to know his father's love and protection. For now, that was enough.

Chapter 3

COOPER STOOD ON THE porch, phone to his ear as he kept watch. The familiar Texas sunset bled crimson over the distant hills, but he took no comfort from the scenic vista tonight. "How soon can you get here?" he rasped into the phone.

Sawyer's voice came through, steady and resolute. "We picked up Viper, and we're already *en route*. ETA fourteen hours if we drive straight through." He sighed. "I wish we'd been able to make the move to Texas happen before now, but with the baby coming, and it taking a while for the owner to get the title issues sorted..."

"I understand, but make it twelve. I'll keep them secure here till you arrive."

"We'll be there, brother. See you soon."

Cooper ended the call and slipped the phone back into his pocket, jaw tense. In the east, the first faint stars had begun to emerge in the dusky sky. Twelve hours. He had to keep Nina and Caleb safe here for twelve more hours alone.

He turned at a scuff of paws behind him. Scooter stood in the open doorway, stub tail wagging. The terrier mix sniffed the air and gave a soft woof. "I know, boy. Trouble's coming." Cooper scratched the dog behind his ears. "We'll be ready."

Scooter leaned into the touch for a moment before trotting back inside. Cooper followed, grabbing his shotgun from where it leaned just inside the door. He moved through the house, checking locks and window latches. In the kitchen, he found Nina rummaging through cabinets.

She turned at his entrance, expression uneasy. "I hope you don't mind. I thought I'd make us some dinner."

Cooper nodded. "Good idea. We'll need to keep our strength up." He eyed the meager ingredients she had set on the counter—a dented can of chili, crackers, and the apples and bread she'd brought. It would have to do for now.

Nina glanced down as if reading his thoughts. "I'm sorry, I don't have much..."

Cooper cut her off. "It's fine. Neither do I. Gotta get to the store sometime, but more supplies are already on the way with my men."

At that, Nina gave him a searching look. "These friends of yours? Can they really protect us from Darren? He has a lot of money, and a lot of power."

Cooper met her eyes levelly. "Doesn't matter. We were Rangers—the best the Army had. Did things most can't even imagine." He hefted the shotgun meaningfully. "Darren should pray he doesn't find out."

She absorbed this silently. In the other room, Caleb made zooming noises as he played. The innocent sound hardened Cooper's resolve. He would lay down his life before he let harm come to the boy.

She turned back to preparing the meager dinner while Cooper continued his security checks. The old ranch house was isolated but defensible, with clear sight lines in all directions. He had ample weapons and ammo stockpiled. Now he just needed bodies to hold the perimeter.

As they ate chili and crackers by candlelight, Cooper maintained watch through the window. The blackness beyond was still and silent. Out there, beyond the thin halo of porch light, Darren's men could even now be making their approach, but the coming hours of darkness belonged to Cooper. He was in his element—the hunted becoming the hunter.

After dinner, he escorted Nina and Caleb to the master suite at the rear of the house. Its single window and solid door made it the most secure room. Nina perched tensely on the edge of the bed while Caleb explored.

He crouched before the boy, hands firm on his skinny shoulders. "I need you and your mama to stay in this room no matter what, okay? Can you do that for me?"

Caleb's dark eyes went round and solemn. He nodded.

He ruffled the boy's hair and stood. Nina rose and moved close, eyes shadowed with fear—for him. The realization landed like a gut punch. She must still care about him in some way.

"Please be careful." Her hand lifted as if to touch his face but fell away without making contact.

Cooper gave a single tight nod. "Lock the door. Don't open it for anything."

Then he turned and left the room before emotion could cripple him. He had a job to do. With ruthless efficiency, he prepared weapons in the kitchen and living area, organizing ammo and supplies, and fortifying vulnerable entry points.

The old floorboards creaked under his weight as he began his vigil, patrolling the house and peering into the darkness. He moved on silent feet honed from years of covert ops. In another life, he had melted into the shadows, striking unseen to eliminate threats. Those lethal instincts rose now again, focused on a single mission—protect his son at any cost.

HOURS LATER, HE SAW the headlights of Mike's Jeep cutting through the darkness and stood up to meet him at the bunkhouse. After that trouble with Kinsey, Mike had stayed "for a spell" to help around the ranch. More than a year later, he still hadn't returned to Chicago, but Sawyer didn't mind.

He left the house after checking on Nina and Caleb, who were both sleeping. Outside, the beams from Cooper's truck cut through the black night as he navigated the rutted dirt road to the old bunkhouse. Mike was already there, having gotten back from his trip to Corpus Christi after Cooper texted him to ask if he'd cut short his trip, but Cooper needed to see for himself that the perimeter was secure.

He pulled up beside Mike's dusty Jeep and killed the engine. The bunkhouse door creaked open, casting a tall silhouette that Cooper would recognize anywhere.

"About time you showed up," Mike drawled as Cooper exited the truck. "Thought I might have to storm the fort alone."

Despite the circumstances, Cooper felt the corner of his mouth twitch. "Not sure you're gonna make it alone. Still have trouble counting past three?"

Mike clutched his chest in mock affront. "And here I was about to offer you a beer. Consider the offer rescinded."

Cooper allowed himself a brief chuckle before turning serious. "Appreciate you coming back early from the big city." Mike was a long-term guest here on the ranch, but he lived his own life, and they sometimes went days without seeing each other. "We need to shore up defenses before Darren's men arrive."

Mike nodded, demeanor shifting seamlessly to business. "Just tell me where you need me."

For the next hour in the bunkhouse, lit by a single bulb, they studied a crude map Cooper had drawn, discussing fields of fire, potential entry points, and positioning. It was a familiar ritual, like old times, and Cooper let himself relax fractionally.

Finally, Mike sat back, scrubbing a hand through his hair. "Think that covers it. We'll give 'em hell when they show their faces." His expression turned curious. "So what's the full deal with this woman and kid? Your text was light on details."

Cooper hesitated, emotions churning inside him that he hardly understood himself. Finally, he gave a truncated version—Nina's past relationship to him, and Caleb's true paternity.

Mike let out a low whistle. "A son, huh? Never figured you for a family man."

Cooper grunted. Family had never been in the cards living the life of a Ranger. He'd walked away from Nina five years ago to keep her from getting entangled. "Wasn't in the cards," he said finally. "Not the life I was living. I liked her a lot. So much that I realized I was in danger of falling for her, and I didn't think I could be a good soldier and a good boyfriend, so I told her it was over at the end of my deployment. I think she hated me a little bit, but she let me go."

"But now?" Mike prodded gently.

Cooper stared at the weathered tabletop, its grain patterns blurred. Since the IED blast that took his leg, he'd built walls around himself as sturdy as this bunkhouse, but Nina and Caleb had come crashing through. "Changes things," he said, the words gravelly in his throat. "At least for me. Can't pretend they're strangers. I hope she doesn't actually hate me." He looked up to meet Mike's eyes. "That boy's mine. My blood. Never thought I'd have that." Emotion roughened his voice.

Mike gripped his shoulder firmly, anchoring him. "You'll figure it out, and we'll make damn sure no one hurts them."

Cooper nodded, jaw tightening with fresh resolve. Mike was right. He didn't know how to be a father yet, but he would do anything to protect Caleb. That had to count for something until they could build a better foundation.

They did a final perimeter check in the truck, bounce of the tires making Cooper's stump ache. He winced as pain lanced through the maimed limb, the ghost of a foot that was no longer there making him grit his teeth. He tuned it out, focusing on scanning the darkness for any signs of intruders.

Finding none, he bid Mike goodnight and headed back to the house, each uneven step a reminder of sacrifices made. Scooter greeted him on the porch, flanked now by Lex.

"Good boys," Cooper murmured. He had allies both canine and human. Come what may in the dark hours ahead, they would face it together. Cooper would defend his family to his final breath if fate demanded, but first, they waited. Watched. Ready.

Chapter 4

NINA LAY AWAKE, LISTENING to the old farmhouse creak and groan around her. Cooper had left her and Caleb barricaded in this back bedroom hours ago, and her nerves strained for any sound of him moving through the house, but only ominous silence reached her ears.

Beside her, Caleb slept soundly, oblivious to the danger that lurked in the darkness outside. Nina envied the peaceful expression on his small face. If only her own mind would allow such respite.

She rose from the bed carefully, not wanting to wake the boy. At the bedroom door, she rested her palm against the solid wood, hesitating. Cooper's parting words echoed in her mind—lock the door, and don't open it for anything.

But the waiting was interminable. She needed to know Cooper was all right. And she needed to pee. With painstaking care, she turned the lock and eased open the door a sliver. The house beyond lay shrouded in shadow. She could just make out Cooper's imposing figure sitting vigil near the front door, shotgun across his knees. His eyes gleamed in the scant moonlight coming through the windows.

Seeing him standing guard eased Nina's anxiety fractionally. She started to ease across the hall to the bathroom when Cooper's head turned, pinning her with his penetrating gaze even through the dark.

She froze. She should close the door and return to the safely of the bedroom as instructed, but her feet seemed rooted in place.

Finally, Cooper broke the tense silence, his voice a gravelly rumble. "You two should be sleeping." Despite the reproach, she detected a note of weariness in his tone.

"I tried. Couldn't turn my mind off." She hesitated. "How are you holding up?"

For a long moment, Cooper just looked at her, his ruined face obscured by shadow. When he responded, his voice was tight. "I'll manage. Long as I know you're secure back there." He shifted his grip on the shotgun meaningfully. "Now get some rest. Can't have you worn out tomorrow when we make our stand."

The unspoken implication being he needed her alert and ready to protect Caleb if Cooper fell tomorrow. The thought chilled her, but Nina just nodded mutely. She lingered a moment more, wishing she could offer some words of comfort or hope, but nothing came, so she darted across the hall to the bathroom, quickly did her business, and returned to the bedroom to ease the door closed once more.

Exhaustion weighed on her as she crawled back under the covers, but her mind still spun, replaying their last moments years ago after Cooper had gotten his deployment orders. She had pleaded with him not to go, terrified each moment could be their last. He had taken her face in both hands, calloused thumbs brushing away her tears, and told her he cared about her, but he couldn't be the man she needed while being a soldier.

She'd been poised to tell him she'd gotten a positive pregnancy test just the day before, but then he'd told her goodbye. Her heart had broken in that instant, and then he was gone, vanished into the Army machine. Until word came, months later, about the explosion that maimed his body and spirit.

She pressed a hand over her eyes, fighting back long-buried grief. If only she had told him about the pregnancy before he deployed, and he'd stayed, or detached from the Army then. Their lives could have been so different.

The bed dipped as Caleb shifted beside her. She looked over at her son, heart swelling. The past Cooper had been cruel to be kind, or so he'd believed, but he was here now when she needed him most. Fate had given them a second chance, however slim. She had to cling to that hope.

NINA MUST HAVE FINALLY dozed, because the next thing she knew, Caleb was shaking her urgently. She came awake with a gasp, heart pounding. Morning light filtered around the blanket Cooper had tacked over the window. She could just make out Caleb's wide eyes and trembling lip.

"Mama, I'm scared." His small voice quavered. "There was a loud boom outside."

Nina's stomach dropped even as she strove to keep her voice calm. "It's okay, baby. Cooper is keeping us safe."

She rose and crossed to peer through a slit in the makeshift curtains. Her pulse roared in her ears. Had Darren's men found them already?

She sagged in relief a moment later as she saw a dusty Jeep pulling up the drive, with a truck close behind. Since Cooper walked out to greet them, she assumed the Cavalry had arrived. They were no longer alone.

"It's Cooper's friends, sweetheart," she assured Caleb, who had come to cling to her leg. "They're here to help."

The rumble of male voices sounded from the other room as the men greeted each other. They spoke in the shorthand of soldiers, their conversation indecipherable, but she could hear the resolve and readiness for battle. She also made out a feminine voice too, which surprised her.

Soon after came a soft tap at the bedroom door before it cracked open. Cooper stood silhouetted against the light from the hallway, his stern expression gentling at the sight of Caleb peeking out from behind Nina's legs.

"My team is here. We're securing the perimeter, and then we'll convene for a briefing." His gravelly voice was all business. "Sit tight. We'll come get you shortly."

Then he was gone again, the door closing firmly behind him. Nina released a pent-up breath. The test was coming, but at least now they had a chance, with stout walls and loyal men standing sentinel. She prayed it would be enough to shield her son from the storm.

A short while later, the bedroom door opened to reveal a young woman Nina didn't recognize. She had warm brown skin, and her dark curls were pulled back in a thick ponytail. One hand rested on her swollen pregnant belly. She gave Nina a tentative smile.

"Hi, there, I'm Kinsey. Sorry to barge in, but Sawyer thought you and your boy could use some breakfast after the long night."

Nina blinked in surprise but quickly recovered. "Thank you. I'm Nina, and this is Caleb." She gestured to where her son still hovered close by her side.

Kinsey beamed at Caleb. "Nice to meet you both. Why don't you come on out, and we'll get you fed?"

Nina followed her to the kitchen, one hand clinging to Caleb's smaller one. Kinsey moved slowly with one hand supporting her pregnant belly.

On the counter sat grocery bags overflowing with bread, eggs, fruit, and other staples. Kinsey began unpacking them, though Nina jumped in to help so the pregnant woman wouldn't have to exert herself.

"The guys really went overboard at the store," said Kinsey with a laugh, holding up the overflowing grocery bags. "I hope you and Caleb like eggs, because it looks like we'll be eating a lot of them."

Nina smiled as she helped Kinsey unpack the food. "Eggs are just fine. Honestly, anything is a treat compared to the gas station snacks we've been living on."

"Well, today you get a real home-cooked breakfast."

As they cooked together, Nina found herself opening up to this sweet pregnant woman, who was clearly beloved by the formidable men here.

"So how did you end up with this crew?" asked Nina. "If you don't mind me asking."

Kinsey smiled, one hand resting on her swollen belly. "It's a bit of a story. I was on the run from my abusive ex when I stumbled into Sawyer's bar one night. He gave me shelter and protection." Her face softened.

"And over time, it became so much more. He's the best thing that ever happened to me."

Nina's heart clenched with emotion. She glanced over at Caleb, who was happily cracking eggs into a bowl. "I think I understand exactly how you feel."

Kinsey followed her gaze and smiled. She squeezed Nina's hand in a gesture of solidarity. In that moment, Nina felt a powerful connection to a kindred spirit. Despite the chaos awaiting them, she was sure she'd found a true friend in Kinsey.

As they cooked and chatted, Nina found herself opening up more about her past. "My parents died when I was young," she said when Kinsey asked. "Car accident. I never had any siblings, so it was just me and my grandfather growing up."

Kinsey's face filled with sympathy. "That must have been so hard losing your parents that way."

Nina nodded, flipping the sizzling potatoes in the pan. "It was, but my grandfather really stepped up to care for me. He was pretty strict, but also loving in his own gruff way." She smiled a little at the memories.

"Sounds like someone else I know," said Kinsey with a knowing look.

Nina chuckled. "Cooper does remind me a little of Grandpa Ed. He was career military too."

She sighed, poking at the potatoes. "Grandpa got sick and passed a couple years back. Since then, it's just been me. Alone until all this trouble..." She trailed off, glancing again at Caleb.

Kinsey touched her arm. "You're not alone anymore. You have us now."

Nina's throat tightened with emotion. She had always relied on herself, being wary of depending on others, but something about this makeshift family Cooper had assembled made her feel like she and Caleb would be okay.

Just then, Caleb trotted over holding up a crayon drawing. "Look, Mama, I drew our family."

Nina's breath caught as she took in the colorful stick figures grouped together on the page—Caleb labeled "Me," Nina labeled "Mama," and Cooper stood apart from them, with two dogs at his side. Her throat was thick with emotion as she took it in, admiring his picture while silently struggling not to cry that he was putting Coop in the picture. It boded well.

Kinsey squeezed Nina's shoulder, both women blinking back tears. "That's going right on the fridge, little man," said Kinsey. She took the drawing and proudly displayed it front and center.

Nina scooped up Caleb for a tight hug, overwhelmed with gratitude for this new extended family protecting them.

Chapter 5

COOPER SURVEYED HIS assembled team, ghosts of old missions swirling through his mind. His brothers-in-arms, bonded by blood and sacrifice. "Appreciate y'all coming." Cooper eyed the tightness in Mike's face as he shifted his braced leg. "How's it holding up?"

"I'm fine." Mike waved him off. "I've logged over fifty kills on this rig. She's got more left in her."

Despite the humor in Mike's voice, Cooper heard the undertone of pain. The doctors said Mike would never walk right again after the blast shredded his leg down to the bone, but here he sat, ready as ever to lay down his life for one more mission.

"Right, here's the situation." Cooper outlined the threat. "What kind of numbers we looking at?"

Sawyer cut right to the heart. "Could be a hit squad, or could be a damn army. This Darren is an unknown."

"He's got money and connections," added Viper, boots kicked up casually on the table. "He'll hit us hard."

Cooper traced a finger over the crude map, uncertainty gnawing at him. He had no recon on what Darren could deploy. The dealer had endless resources and criminal contacts, and he was motivated to silence Nina at all costs.

"There's always a way. We just have to find it." Cooper met each man's gaze. "I'll take any crazy idea right now."

Mike grinned. "Well, crazy ideas are our specialty, right, boys?"

Fond memories flashed through Cooper's mind. Mike hotwiring vehicles in the middle of firefights. Sawyer "borrowing" enemy trucks to move equipment. Viper improvising explosives from fertilizer and kerosene. Crazy kept them alive when the odds were suicidal. Which they often were.

"We need to control the battlefield." Sawyer pointed out choke points on the map. "Canalize them into kill zones."

They descended into the familiar rhythms of analysis and debate. Hours fell away as possibilities took shape, plans formed and contingencies stacked. In these moments, past and present merged into a seamless tapestry of purpose.

"It'll be ugly, no way around that," said Cooper finally, "But our priority is zero casualties." His gaze flicked to the closed door behind which his makeshift family sheltered. "The main priority is protecting Nina, Caleb, and Kinsey."

Sawyer sighed. "I tried to talk her out of coming, but she was determined."

"Nina needs a friend right now. It's good she's here."

Mike clapped his shoulder. "Sounds like we've got ourselves a fighting chance." His eyes glinted with optimism. "Hell, Darren should pray he stays far from this hornet's nest."

As the others readied to disperse, Cooper cleared his throat. "Whatever happens, I appreciate you coming." His voice rasped with emotion. "Couldn't do this without you."

Sawyer clasped his shoulder, expression solemn. "We go where the fight is, but this one's personal too." His eyes held understanding.

Mike groaned as he stood. "Let's save the Hallmark moment. You know we've got your six, Coop."

"I don't know. I'm feeling all warm and fuzzy over here," Viper added with exaggerated emotion, clutching his heart.

Cooper snorted, the brief levity easing his spirit. "How about you warm up that trigger finger instead?"

He watched them file out with fresh resolve. The coming days promised bloodshed and hardship, but his brothers would stand with him, bonded by loyalty stronger than steel. Together, they would defend this family to their last breaths.

LATER THAT NIGHT, COOPER stood solitary vigil on the porch, shotgun across his knees. The distant hills were bathed in moonlight, a deceptive tranquility masking the violence soon to descend upon them.

He tensed at the creak of the screen door opening behind him. Then he heard Nina's voice, soft and hesitant in the darkness. "Mind if I join you?"

Cooper grunted assent, eyes still scanning the perimeter. She settled quietly beside him in the old rocking chair, drawing her sweater tighter against the night's chill. For several minutes, only the low chirring of crickets broke the silence. Then Nina spoke, voice barely above a whisper. "Thank you. For everything you're doing...for us."

Cooper shifted in his seat, discomfort prickling his neck. "You don't need to thank me. I'm just..."

"Protecting what's yours?" Nina finished when he trailed off. Amusement lurked beneath her words.

He cleared his throat, recalling his brusque declaration earlier. He hadn't missed her reaction to the word "mine." There was too much left unsaid between them. "I didn't mean to presume—" he began gruffly.

"You're not." Nina's hand lifted as if to touch his arm, then fell away. "Whatever happens...I'm glad we found each other again. That Caleb will know his father, even for a little while."

Emotion thickened Cooper's throat. In the dark, ghosts swirled—moments shared between them those years ago in this very spot. All turned to ash in an instant by his choices and harsh fate. "I should have written. Reached out, after..." He didn't have to explain when after meant. The day that changed everything, turning the man he was to dust.

Nina was silent for a long moment. "We both made choices then. Right or wrong, we can't go back." When she continued, her voice was fragile as spun glass. "But we're here now."

The unspoken words shimmered between them. Here, now, with a second chance dangling before them—however slender and fragile that chance might be with Darren's threats looming.

Cooper clutched his weapon tighter, palms suddenly slick. Could have beens warred with harsh reality in his mind. Futures glimpsed and lost. His failings as a man, as a soldier, as a father, haunted him.

"Will you tell Caleb..." His throat closed around the words. Tell Caleb what? That his father had tried? Loved him in whatever broken way he could?

Nina's hand found his now, warm and trembling. "You'll tell him yourself. When this is over." There was steel in her voice now, willing the possibility into being through sheer force of hope.

Cooper looked down at their entwined fingers, tanned against golden-brown, his callouses caressing her smooth skin. The touch ignited a spark inside long left cold, a flame of longing and desire he'd never allowed himself to feel. Not since that last day together under this boundless sky.

Nina must have sensed it too and felt the kindling heat between them. She leaned closer, eyes searching his, until only inches separated them. For endless suspended moments they lingered there, caught on the precipice of irrevocable change.

Then Cooper pulled back, breaking the spell. His body screamed in protest even as warning klaxons sounded in his mind. Not now. Not yet. "We need rest." It came out hoarser than intended. "Long days ahead. Get some sleep."

She drew in a shuddering breath, disappointment playing at the corners of her mouth, but she rose without protest, pausing at the screen door to glance back. "Goodnight, Cooper." Her eyes shone with emotion in the darkness before she slipped inside.

Cooper released a pent-up breath, his gut churning. As he stared sightlessly into the night, one yearning thought echoed ceaselessly through his mind. If they survived this crucible, could the ghosts of the past finally rest? And could new hope dawn in their place?

A creak of floorboards behind him broke Cooper from his brooding thoughts. He turned to see Mike easing out onto the porch, two glasses and a bottle of whiskey in hand.

"Thought you could use a drink," he said, dropping into the rocking chair Nina had vacated. He splashed whiskey into the glasses and passed one to Cooper.

Cooper accepted it with a grateful nod. The liquor's slow burn soothed his jangled nerves as they drank in silence for several minutes, passing the bottle back and forth.

"This is probably a bad idea. I spent too much time in the bottle after the accident," Cooper finally rumbled, gaze fixed on the darkness ahead.

Mike nodded. "Same. I'm careful about how much I drink now, but it's a night that calls for it." He shifted his braced leg with a faint wince Cooper pretended not to notice. "She seems like a good woman. Nina," he said after another swallow of whiskey. "Her and the boy."

Cooper stared down at the amber liquid in his glass, emotions roiling. Mike had always been able to read him, even when words failed.

"Never expected to have a family," Cooper admitted finally, gravelly voice nearly lost on the night breeze. "Now that I do..."

He shook his head helplessly. The future had never held possibilities like these, like love, fatherhood, or things far beyond just duty and honor. After the IED, his life had promised to be one of struggle and pain, and he'd figured he'd never put that burden on someone else. He'd resigned himself to being alone and hardly knew how to hold such fragile hopes, yet he would fight like hell to keep them.

Mike leaned forward intently. "You'll figure it out, brother. We've got your back." His certainty helped anchor Cooper against the storm of doubts and fears.

They drank awhile longer in companionable silence until Mike clapped Cooper's shoulder and stood. "Try to get some shut eye. I'll take next watch."

Cooper nodded, standing slowly on legs gone stiff. He winced as the prosthetic slid slightly, putting extra pressure on his stump until he adjusted his gait.As Mike disappeared into the darkness, Cooper lingered a moment more. Somewhere beyond the darkness, morning waited, and with it, a future he now dared to dream of. Gripping that hope close, Cooper turned and entered the house.

Chapter 6

MORNING SUNLIGHT FILTERING through the curtains woke Nina from restless dreams. She rose and dressed quietly, not wanting to disturb Caleb still curled under his blankets, dark hair mussed across the pillow.

In the kitchen, sizzling bacon and percolating coffee filled the air. Kinsey stood at the stove flipping pancakes, the task made awkward by her heavily pregnant belly. Despite the bright smile Kinsey flashed, Nina noticed the puffy shadows under her eyes. They were all fraying at the edges as the danger approached.

"Morning. Hungry?" Kinsey didn't wait for an answer, already loading a plate high with pancakes and bacon and placing it at the table.

Her stomach growled, suddenly ravenous at the sight of food. "Starving. This smells amazing."

They carried platters laden with eggs, bacon, and pancakes to the dining table just as the men began shuffling inside, drawn by the aromas of breakfast. Nina's pulse stuttered when Cooper entered, his stern face softening almost imperceptibly at the sight of her. The very air between them seemed charged by their unvoiced attraction.

Nina busied herself pouring coffee, hyper aware of Cooper's every movement though they didn't speak. She nearly sloshed hot liquid over her hand when his fingers accidentally brushed hers taking the mug from her trembling grip.

After everyone was served, Cooper cleared his throat, all business again. "We'll continue preparations today. Fortify weak points, stash supplies, and set traps." His flinty tone made clear he expected nothing less than full effort from every person present.

The group dispersed shortly after eating, the men heading out to continue strengthening defenses while Nina helped Kinsey clear the table. As they washed dishes side-by-side, Caleb wandered over to tug at Nina's shirt.

"Mama, can we go see the cows today?" His small face was hopeful.

Nina hesitated. She knew Cooper wanted them inside, away from any potential threats, but Caleb's pleading eyes eroded her resistance.

"I suppose a short walk wouldn't hurt, but we have to stay close, okay?"

Caleb nodded eagerly and pulled her toward the front door. Out on the porch, Nina nearly collided with Cooper's broad chest as he exited. She drew up short, pulse kicking.

Cooper frowned down at them. "Where are you two off to?"

"Just a quick walk to see the cows. Caleb's request." Nina touched her son's shoulder, feeling suddenly defensive under Cooper's stern gaze.

Cooper seemed to war with himself before finally nodding. "Fine, but stay in sight of the house, and take this." He held out a small radio. "Any sign of trouble, you radio me right away, got it?"

"Of course." Nina clipped the radio to her belt, absurdly touched by his protectiveness. She took Caleb's hand and they set off across the pasture.

They enjoyed their brief outing, Caleb giggling with delight as the curious cows ambled over to inspect them, but Nina stayed hyper alert, one hand on the radio at her hip. The pleasant interlude ended too quickly. Back inside the fortified house, Nina couldn't shake a creeping sense of dread.

OVER THE NEXT COUPLE of days, they settled into an anxious routine—the men laboring tirelessly to prepare defenses while Nina and Kinsey handled domestic tasks, since neither of them had combat experience. It felt wrong to have them assuming all the risk, but when she and Kinsey lacked the necessary skills, it would be stupid to put everyone in danger just to defray some of the risk from the men.

Mealtimes brought them together, though conversation was sparse with the looming threat hanging over all their heads. In the evenings, Caleb begged Cooper to read with him. Nina's heart swelled watching them together on the couch, two heads bent intently over a storybook. Her son was opening up more to his father each day, soaking up the paternal affection he'd missed.

Scooter had attached himself to Caleb, scarcely leaving the boy's side even to sleep. The terrier followed Caleb everywhere as though patrolling for any dangers. Though the ranch was secured, Scooter seemed ready to confront any threat to his young charge.

Nina was deeply grateful for the fierce devotion both father and furry companion were developing to her son. She could only pray it would be enough when Darren's malice inevitably arrived at their doorstep.

Her own relationship with Cooper remained tentative, filled with emotionally charged moments neither was ready to confront, but Nina cherished each miracle minute they all had together as a fledgling family, no matter how precarious their future.

Late one evening, Nina slipped out onto the porch craving a quiet moment alone with her thoughts. She tensed when the screen door creaked open behind her, then relaxed slightly at the familiar raspy voice.

"Mind if I join you?" Cooper's imposing figure filled the doorway, his face etched with new lines from the day's labors.

Nina shook her head, pulse quickening as Cooper came to stand beside her at the railing. This was the first time they'd been alone since their moonlit talk nights ago. The night air fairly crackled with unspoken feelings hanging between them.

They stood without speaking, the silence weighted with emotions neither was ready to voice. Then Cooper reached into his shirt pocket and withdrew a folded paper.

"Caleb made this for you earlier." He held it out to her.

Nina unfolded it to reveal a crayon drawing of two stick figures holding hands, one large and one small. Love for her son welled up, momentarily choking her voice.

"It's beautiful," she finally managed. "He's so creative."

"Takes after his mama," Cooper said roughly.

Nina glanced up to find him watching her, eyes dark and fathomless in the dim light. Her breath stalled.

"Cooper..." She trailed off, uncertain what she wanted to say, what she wanted from him in this moment.

A sudden shrill beep from the radio at Nina's hip made them both jump. Fumbling it off her belt with a racing heart, Nina listened to Mike's terse message that changed everything.

"They're coming. Leaving town now. Be there within the hour."

The breath died in Nina's throat. The drawing slipped from her numb fingers as icy fear gripped her insides. This was it. The fight was upon them.

She looked at Cooper and saw hard purpose settle on his craggy features even as he gripped her shoulder bracingly.

"Get inside and stay with Caleb," he ordered. "We're as ready as can be."

Then he was striding away, already barking orders into his radio, rallying the ranch's defenders. Nina drew a shuddering breath and turned to follow, Caleb's drawing lying forgotten on the weathered boards. However inadequate their preparations felt now, they had no choice but to see this through. For her son's sake, she had to believe it was enough.

Inside, she found Caleb playing on the living room rug. At the sight of her stricken face, he froze, his small brow creasing in confusion and worry.

"Mama? What's wrong?"

Nina quickly composed her features, forcing an unconcerned smile. "Nothing, baby. Come help me in the kitchen."

She glanced out the window as they walked, glimpsing armed men running to take up positions in the coming battle. Fear clawed at her, but she choked it down. She had to be strong for Caleb.

In the kitchen, she pretended to tidy up, keeping up a stream of chatter to occupy Caleb's attention. His rapt expression told her the ruse was working. For now.

Gunshots erupted suddenly outside, making them both jump. Caleb's eyes went wide with alarm. "What was that, Mama?"

Instead of answering, she diverted. "Let's read some stories to drown it out." She took him to the master bedroom, fortifying it as best as she could before pulling him down onto the floor with her.

He frowned. "Why can't we lay down?"

She wanted the mattress protecting their backs, but she couldn't tell him that. Instead, she grabbed a blanket at put it over them. "Because this is a fort, sweetie."

After a moment of skepticism, he let himself be swayed by the book they were reading. She spent the next agonizing stretch of time immersed in picture books, straining to hear any sounds hinting at how the battle progressed. At last the gunfire tapered off, then went silent. Nina held her breath, braced for whatever came next.

Heavy boots sounded on the porch, then the front door banged open. Nina jumped up, placing herself between Caleb and the door.

Relief crashed over her at the sight of Cooper striding inside, streaked with dust but unharmed. Their eyes met, and Nina saw her own bone-deep exhaustion reflected there, but they had survived. Against all odds, they were still standing.

For now, that was enough.

"You can come out for now," he said a tad gruffly before turning and walking down the hallway.

Chapter 7

COOPER STOOD IN THE open doorway, surveying the bullet-pocked exterior of the ranch house. Darren's men had retreated for now, but they'd inflicted damage. Next time would be worse.

Footsteps sounded behind him, then Nina's voice, rich with relief. "Is it over?"

Cooper turned, seeing cautious hope in her eyes. He wished he could erase the new worry lines from her face. "We held them off." He kept his voice steady. "But this was just the first wave."

Nina paled, one hand covering her mouth. Cooper ached to pull her close, comfort her, but harsh truths remained. "Darren won't quit. He'll keep attacking with more men and more weapons." Jaw tightening, Cooper met her frightened gaze. "We have to end this. Permanently."

Nina's eyes widened. "What do you mean?"

"We'll figure out a plan."

Nina absorbed this silently before giving a single tight nod. She seemed dismayed that he didn't have an immediate answer for her. He was nonplussed too. Darren would keep chipping away at their defenses, but at least it was over for tonight.

Bone-tired after that battle, Cooper stood under the streaming shower a couple of hours later, letting the hot water sluice away the dirt and tension. He tensed at the sound of the bathroom door opening over the patter of spray. Then Nina's voice, soft but firm. "It's just me. Don't be alarmed."

Cooper froze as the shower curtain slid back. She stood bare before him, eyes vulnerable but determined.

"Nina..." Cooper rasped in surprise. "What are you doing?"

"What I should have done that night on the porch." She stepped closer, never breaking eye contact. "If tomorrow ends in flames, I don't want to have missed this chance."

The breath left Cooper's lungs. Nina's lips met his, tentative at first, then more urgent. Cooper gave himself to the kiss, pouring every bottled-up emotion into it as the water sluiced down their entwined bodies.

Finally he broke the kiss, cupping her face in both hands. "There will be a tomorrow for us," he vowed gruffly. "I swear it."

Nina just pulled him close once more. Her lips crashed over his, and she kissed him with a ferocity that stole his breath.

Their tongues tangled, and Cooper groaned, pulling her flush against him. His cock hardened instantly, pressing into the softness of her belly.

She gasped, grinding against him, and Cooper growled, lifting her up onto his lap, where he sat on the built-in shower chair. He hated showering with his prosthetic leg and was glad to have the chair to support both of them.

"Oh," Nina cried out in surprise, but she didn't protest. Instead, she wrapped her legs around his waist, straddling him.

Cooper's cock throbbed, aching to be inside her slick heat, but he forced himself to slow down. This was their first time after so long apart, and he wanted to savor every moment.

He trailed kisses down her neck, nipping at the sensitive skin and making her shiver. Her breasts were pressed against his chest, and he reached up to cup them, teasing her nipples into stiff peaks. "They're bigger than I remember."

She smiled, looking a little embarrassed. "Pregnancy and breastfeeding will do that."

Cooper grinned, leaning forward to capture one brown nipple in his mouth. He sucked gently, swirling his tongue around the sensitive bud.

Nina moaned, arching her back and pushing her breast deeper into his mouth. Cooper continued to suck, alternating between her two breasts until she was writhing in his arms.

"Please, Cooper. I need to touch you." She reached down, wrapping her fingers around his thick shaft.

Cooper hissed at the sensation, bucking his hips involuntarily. Her touch was like fire, sending sparks of pleasure shooting through his body.

He released her nipple, capturing her mouth in a searing kiss but froze when her hand glided down his stump. When he stiffened, she hesitated. "Should I stop?"

Cooper swallowed hard, fighting the urge to hide his amputated limb. "No. It's okay. I just... I'm still getting used to it and haven't been with anyone in nearly five years... You were my last lover before deployment and the IED." He rested his forehead against hers, and her damp curls clung to his forehead. "I'm sorry I'm so self-conscious, but I've never felt so exposed."

"You're beautiful, Cooper. Every part of you." Her words were fierce, and her eyes burned with sincerity. "Let me show you how much I love every inch of you."

With that, she leaned forward and began kissing his scarred face that he found so monstrous when he looked in the mirror now. She kissed the jagged line across his cheekbone, the puckered flesh of his ear, and the twisted knot of tissue near his temple where shrapnel had embedded.

Cooper's eyes closed as he surrendered to her touch, allowing himself to feel each brush of her lips against his damaged skin. Her fingers traced the raised ridges of his scars, and he shuddered at the sensation. Her acceptance and desire made him feel whole again, and he would never be able to let her go.

Her lips moved to his neck, her tongue tracing the line of ragged scar tissue there. It wasn't uncomfortable, but it wasn't entirely pleasurable. Still, he didn't object, understanding she wanted to prove something to him.

When she moved lower, trailing kisses down his shoulder and chest, he gasped, his cock hardening even more. Her mouth was warm and wet, and she licked the sensitive skin around his nipple before sucking it into her mouth.

Cooper groaned, tangling his fingers in her thick curls. Her tongue swirled around his nipple, sending bolts of pleasure straight to his groin.

She continued her exploration, moving lower until she reached the scar on his belly, where the doctor had taken skin to graft onto his stump. Her tongue traced the length of the scar, and Cooper shivered at the sensation. It was strange but not unpleasant.

His cock twitched, and he waited for her to take it into her mouth. Instead, with a small smile, she licked down his thigh, stopping near the end of his stump. He stiffened, unable to help the reaction.

"Relax," she said softly, stroking the inside of his thigh. "Trust me."

Cooper took a deep breath, forcing himself to relax. He knew she wouldn't hurt him, but it was difficult to let go of his inhibitions.

As if sensing his hesitation, Nina continued to stroke his inner thigh, massaging the tense muscles. Her fingers brushed against his balls, and he moaned, his cock throbbing with need.

"That feels good." He murmured, closing his eyes as she continued to massage his thighs.

Her fingers moved higher, brushing against the base of his cock and making him gasp before trailing back down again. A featherlight touch of her fingertips stroking his stump made him tremble.

"Does that feel good?" Her voice was low and husky, filled with desire.

"Yes." He managed to choke out, barely recognizing his own voice. "I never expected that area to feel good again. Or to be touched like this. Otherwise, it's just me or the doctor. The physical therapist at the VA in the beginning..."

"Shh." Her fingers continued to trace patterns on his stump, and he moaned as she pressed harder, increasing the pressure.

"Nina, please." He was desperate for release, his cock aching with need. It had been so long since he'd been touched like this, and he couldn't hold back any longer.

"What do you need, Cooper?" Her voice was a seductive whisper, and he could hear the smile in her tone.

"I need you." He growled, reaching for her. "I need to be inside you."

She laughed softly, taking his shaft in her hand and guiding it to her dripping center. The head of his cock nudged at her entrance, and he groaned as she slowly sank down onto him.

Her tight heat enveloped him, and he gripped her hips, thrusting up into her. They moved together, finding a rhythm that brought them both pleasure. It registered dimly in the back of his mind that they weren't using protection, but he couldn't bring himself to stop. So what if he got her pregnant again? This time, he'd be there for it all instead of spending the first four years of his child's life without knowing he had a son.

He thrust harder, burying himself to the hilt inside her. She cried out, digging her nails into his shoulders as she rode him. Her breasts bounced with each movement, and he reached up to cup them, tweaking her nipples.

"Oh, Cooper, I've missed this." She moaned, throwing her head back as she ground against him. "Don't stop."

He had no intention of stopping, not when she felt so incredible around him. Her walls clenched around his shaft, and he knew she was close, her body trembling with the effort to hold back her orgasm. He was close too, and he thrust harder, driving into her with wild abandon as he reached between them to rub her clit.

"Come for me, Nina. I want to feel you come around my cock." He growled, pinching her clit just enough to send her over the edge.

She screamed, her muscles clamping around him as her climax hit. The sensation was enough to push him over the edge, and he came with a roar, spilling himself inside her.

They collapsed against each other, panting and sweaty as the water continued to rain down around them. Cooper held her close, stroking her hair as they caught their breath.

"I can't believe it's been so long since we did that. If I'd realized how it would be, I'd have taken you to bed the first night you arrived." She kissed his most scarred cheek as she said the words.

"I didn't think you'd want to. Not after everything that happened, and I was so angry. Angry at myself, at the world, at the universe, and you for not telling me about Caleb." He sucked in a deep breath, feeling his cock stiffen again inside her when she shifted slightly. "I didn't think you'd want...this anyway. I'm half the man I used to be."

"You're still a man, Cooper. A damn fine one, and I've always wanted you. Even when you were gone, I dreamed of your return. Of being in your arms again. I just thought you'd never forgive me. Never want to see me again when you didn't answer my letter about being pregnant."

She bit her lip. "I should have written more than one, but I was so sure you'd reject Caleb after you broke up with me before you shipped out. 'Service and relationships don't mix.'" Her tone was bitter as she quoted back his own words to him, said five years ago when he made the decision to end it before going on his next deployment.

"I was wrong. I was scared. I thought I'd get distracted by the relationship and endanger my team. It was a stupid excuse, but I didn't believe I could be a good Ranger and a good boyfriend. I thought I had to choose." He sighed, stroking her hair and kissing her forehead. "I'm sorry I was such an idiot. I wish I'd known. I would have been here for you and Caleb. I would have married you."

"Would you?" Her eyes searched his, and he saw the vulnerability in them. "Even though you'd already told me you didn't do commitment?"

"I was young and dumb. I thought I had to choose between the Army and a family. Now, I know better. I'd marry you in a heartbeat, Nina. I love you. I've always loved you. Nothing's changed that." He felt open and vulnerable making the admission, because the odds were, her feelings had altered drastically in five years. Just because she still desired him—which was a miracle in his current state—didn't mean she still loved him.

"I love you too, Cooper. I never stopped loving you. I tried, but I couldn't. I even dated a few guys, but I couldn't make myself fall in love with anyone else. You're the only one for me." Tears welled in her eyes, and he wiped them away with his thumb.

"Then it's settled. We'll get married as soon as this is over. I'll make an honest woman of you." He grinned, trying to lighten the mood.

She laughed, sniffing back tears. "I'd like that, but I don't want to rush into anything. Let's wait until we're safe. Until we're free of Darren. Then we can talk about marriage."

Cooper nodded, although he was disappointed. He wanted to make her his wife as soon as possible but understood her reluctance. There was still a lot of danger ahead, and she needed to focus on keeping herself and Caleb safe.

"Okay, but I want you to know, I'm serious. I want to spend the rest of my life with you. I want to be a father to Caleb. I want us to be a family." He cupped her face in his hands, gazing into her eyes. "I promise, I'll keep you safe. I'll protect you and Caleb with my life. I won't let Darren or anyone else hurt you."

"I know. I trust you, Cooper. I always have, even when I thought you hated me. I knew you'd keep Caleb safe." She kissed him, and he lost himself in the sweetness of her lips. "We should probably get out of the shower before we use up all the hot water." She finally pulled away, smiling up at him. "Other people might want to shower too."

He made his cock twitch inside her, which caused her to moan. "We can spare five more minutes," he said with a husky chuckle.

Chapter 8

MORNING SUNLIGHT FILTERING through the curtains stirred Nina awake. For a moment she languished in the warm cocoon of Cooper's embrace, their bare skin still entwined. Memories of last night enveloped her. The wordless joining of their bodies and hearts that had shifted everything between them.

Reluctantly disengaging from the solid muscle of his arms, she rose and dressed, movements slow and pleasantly sore. She paused in the bedroom doorway to glance back. Cooper still slept, face softened and years younger, dark hair falling over his forehead. Emotion clogged Nina's throat at this rare unguarded glimpse. Unable to resist, she returned to the bedside to brush a feather-light kiss over his stubbled cheek before slipping out.

In the kitchen, rich scents of coffee and sizzling bacon filled the air. Nina found Kinsey already there, one hand braced on the small of her back for support while the other awkwardly maneuvered a cast iron skillet on the stovetop. Her rotund belly clearly threw off her balance.

"Here, let me help with that," she said, rushing over to take the heavy pan before Kinsey could strain herself.

"You're a lifesaver, thanks." Kinsey flashed her a tired smile, though it didn't quite erase the smudges under her eyes. The attack had frazzled all their nerves.

"Where were you last night, when the attack started?"

"I was in the bunkhouse. Sawyer shoved me into the storm shelter." She grimaced. "There are so many spiders down there."

"Yuck. They're good for the environment, but you should share the bedroom with me and Caleb...next time." There it was. The bald admission that Darren would be back.

"I will if I'm close enough." Her tired eyes reflected the same fear Nina felt.

Working side-by-side, they prepared a hearty breakfast. As Nina fried eggs and potatoes, Kinsey sliced fruit while sitting at the table. Their easy camaraderie soothed Nina's lingering anxiety from recent events.

"Have you thought of any names yet?" she asked, gesturing to Kinsey's belly.

Kinsey laughed softly, one hand cradling the bump protectively. "A few ideas, but Sawyer and I go back and forth. We have a bet going on if it's a boy or girl. I say girl, and he's convinced it's a boy." Her face glowed with maternal joy and anticipation. "He wanted to find out, but I want to be surprised."

Nina's heart swelled. Not long ago, her own future had seemed dim and uncertain. Now, new paths were unfolding she'd never imagined.

Their conversation flowed easily as they prepared platters of food. Details of nursery colors and baby shower plans momentarily overshadowed the violence still lurking beyond these walls. For now, Nina cherished the illusion of normalcy.

Soon, the men filtered into the kitchen, drawn by the rich aromas, and Caleb joined them too. Their shoulders seemed to relax fractionally breathing in the scents of home and comfort, but Nina noticed they all took seats facing the room's entrances, instinct not yet allowing them to fully stand down. She wondered how long they could maintain their edge before exhaustion caught up, and adrenaline flagged.

"We have to take the fight to him," said Cooper suddenly.

She stiffened. "What?"

"It's the only way to end this," said Mike.

"We've been in contact with a friend of ours. Former commander, Clayton, who tells us Darren is being investigated by the IRS. Unfortunately, that's moving at glacial pace, and not that many IRS investigations lead to guns blazing and taking out the bad guys, so it's up to us." Cooper sounded resigned.

"No, that's crazy. It'd be suicide." Nina shook her head, gripping Coop's forearm. "You can't."

"We have to. Clayton got us some good intel. It'll take us a few days to prepare, but this is the way forward. The best...only...way to protect Caleb."

She closed her eyes, warring with herself before finally nodding. She opened her eyes again. "If you think it's for the best, I trust you."

"We're not going off half-cocked," said Viper. "We'll be safe and smart, which is why it'll take us a few days to plan."

She nodded, trying to hide her fear. It struck her as crazy, but they'd survived terrible things, so she'd place her trust in the brotherhood.

IN THE DAYS THAT FOLLOWED, Nina existed in a state of heightened unease. Darren had gone ominously silent since his last failed attack, surely planning his next brutal blow. Nina forced herself to remain focused, helping prepare medical supplies and provisions they would need when he returned.

When the attack finally came, Nina was bent over a raised bed of herbs in the garden when the sharp crack of gunfire shattered the stillness. She dove for cover, heart lurching. This was no long-distance sniper assault. Figures emerged from the treeline on foot, spraying the house with a barrage of bullets.

Chaos erupted. Nina scrambled back inside, nearly colliding with Kinsey as they rushed to grab Caleb then take shelter in the fortified storm cellar. Huddled in the earthen darkness, surrounded by spiders, they clung to each other. The outside assault was reduced to muffled booms. Each minute crawled by agonizingly until at last the shooting tapered off, then ceased.

Nina crept back into the ransacked house cautiously, squinting as her eyes adjusted to the sunlight streaming through shattered windows. Miraculously their group seemed mostly unscathed, though grim determination had replaced the easy camaraderie at breakfast. A bullet had grazed Sawyer's upper arm, but when Nina rushed to help tend the injury, he waved off the ministrations.

"It's just a scratch. I've had worse." Jaw clenched against the pain, Sawyer flexed his fingers to check his weapon's grip. His eyes flashed like steel. "We move on Darren's dealership tomorrow as planned. This ends now."

Ice trickled down Nina's spine at his words, but she squared her shoulders and lifted her chin. She would place her trust in Cooper and follow wherever he led.

That night, Nina lay awake long after Caleb's breaths evened into sleep. Worries nipped at the edges of her mind like hungry wolves. Could they succeed at extracting the evidence from under Darren's nose? Getting proof was the only way to stop Darren from coming after her. They needed to give him bigger problems to focus on, but what casualties might they sustain?

The last thought pierced Nina's heart. She turned over to look at him. His small form was just visible, tucked amid stuffed animals and blankets. Nina smoothed back his unruly curls and place a light kiss on his forehead.

"I love you, my sweet boy," she whispered into the darkness. "Be brave."

Whether their desperate gambit tomorrow failed or succeeded, she would go to the ends of the earth to protect this precious child. He was her reason for breathing, for fighting on despite impossible odds. She would see peace restored, so her son could grow and thrive, unafraid.

On silent feet, she rose and left the bedroom, finding Cooper in the living room, sacked out on the couch. She climbed in beside him, rolling into his waiting arms. He shifted but didn't wake as Nina settled her head over his heart, drawing comfort from its steady rhythm.

Tomorrow, he might die trying to save her and Caleb. If these were to be their last stolen hours, Nina was grateful to spend them cradled against Cooper's strength.

Chapter 9

PREDAWN LIGHT SEEPED through the blinds as Cooper meticulously inspected each weapon—

field-stripping, oiling, and reassembling. Today, they invaded the Darren's lair to find the evidence needed to bury the shithead for good. His gut roiled with tension, but his hands remained steady, repeating motions ingrained through endless drills.

Behind him, soft footfalls sounded on the hardwood floor, then Nina's sleep-roughened voice. "I should go with you."

Cooper swiveled to face her, taking in the determined set of her jaw even as lurking fear shadowed her eyes. His chest tightened. "No. I need you here, protecting Caleb."

Nina's spine straightened stubbornly. "Kinsey can watch him just fine. You need every person who can hold a gun."

Cooper stepped closer, ducking his head to meet her gaze, willing her to understand. "This is war, Nina. I can't be second-guessing your position or safety in the chaos."

"I won't be a liability, I swear it—" Desperation tinged her voice now.

Cooper cut her off, hands firm on her shoulders. "You being there at all is liability enough, don't you see?" At her stricken look, he softened his tone. "Please. Guard our son. Leave the fighting to those of us with the skills. Please."

The words seemed to sink like stones between them. Nina clearly longed to argue further, but finally she dipped her chin in reluctant acquiescence. Cooper released a breath, pulling her closer and savoring each shared heartbeat. Whatever awaited him today, this was no goodbye.

Too soon, he forced himself to straighten, locking down wayward emotions. "We've got one shot at this. Everybody know the plan?"

Sawyer flicked open a butterfly knife, spinning it in agile fingers. "Get in quick and quiet, access the safe, and get the evidence to pass along to Clayton. Clean and easy."

As if anything about this would be easy, but Cooper layered his voice with artificial confidence. "Exactly. Let's load up."

The drive into Houston was tense, every sense primed for signs of ambush, but they reached the dealership seemingly unchallenged. Still, hard-earned caution slowed their exit from the vehicles. Weapons up, safeties off, they approached the gleaming showroom like specters. It was Sunday afternoon, and the place was closed so Darren could pretend to be a good citizen and be seen attending church.

Clayton said word was, the man had political aspirations once his illegal actions built up his coffers enough to run. Made sense. Most politicians were just criminals in suits to Coop's way of thinking.

Upstairs, Cooper stationed himself at the junction of two hallways while Viper set to work disabling the security systems. From around a corner came a sudden scuffle of boots. They weren't alone here. Cooper flashed hand signals for silence as his team froze, senses razor-edged.

Moments later, two armed guards rounded the bend. Cooper and Sawyer seized them from behind before they could cry out, applying brutal, efficient force to leave the men unconscious but breathing. After dragging the limp bodies out of sight, they continued their stealthy advance toward the inner sanctum.

Viper soon had the heavy oak door open. Heart thudding, Cooper led the way into the darkened office, gun sweeping for targets. The room was still and silent but for a lingering odor of fine cigars.

"Watch the door," Cooper told Mike tersely. "We make this quick and clean."

He moved swiftly to the massive desk and began rifling through drawers while Sawyer set a targeted charge to blow the hidden wall safe.

Each second crawled by, seeming an eternity as they hunted the damning evidence that would spell Darren's ruin.

Echoing shouts sounded from beyond the door. Mike spun from his guard position. "Company."

No more time for niceties. Sawyer blew the safe, and they grabbed everything inside, scanning documents as exploded plaster still rained down around them. They appeared to be a treasure trove of shipping logs, bank accounts, and customer lists from a cursory look.

"Got it, now move out," barked Cooper. They surged from the office in unison. Down the hallway, approaching boots pounded as guards raced to intercept.

Gunfire erupted, rounds chewing the walls above their heads as they ran the gauntlet. Ricochets screamed past their ears, but somehow, all found their marks. They plunged into the stairwell and down the concrete steps three at a time, bursting through a side door into the alley's gloomy damp.

Tires shrieked as Mike pulled up. They dove into the truck while attempting to return fire. Then they were roaring away into the later afternoon, the dealership in shambles behind them. Against all odds, they had done it. They had secured the prize Darren would have, and probably had, killed to protect. His reign ended today.

Still jittery with adrenaline, Cooper scanned their surroundings relentlessly as they sped toward sanctuary. The streets around them remained empty. No tails emerged from the darkness in pursuit. After driving around for a while, assuring they had no tail, Mike took them back in the direction of the ranch.

NINA MET THEM ON THE porch, descending the steps like avenging angel to throw her arms around Cooper's neck. As her relieved tears dampened his shirt, the last of the day's tension eased from his bones. "We made it happen in broad daylight," he told her with a cocky grin, though it felt a little wobbly around the edges.

The distant thrum of helicopter blades made them break their embrace. Cooper tensed, fingers tightening on his rifle stock before he recognized the black chopper emblazoned with official seals as it came in low over the ranch.

Clayton jumped down before the skids even touched dirt, striding toward them. His crisp uniform and close-cropped silver hair left no doubt he was here in an official capacity. "Got your message you have something for me." Clayton extended a hand to Cooper, who shook it firmly.

"Hope we didn't pull you from anything urgent."

Clayton's mouth quirked. "Let's just say, certain powers are highly invested in seeing Mr. Silva's enterprises shut down." His sharp gaze took in the group. "But that depends on what you managed to retrieve."

In response, Sawyer held up a thick manila envelope. "Shipping logs, bank records, and offshore accounts from what I saw during the drive back. Everything needed to dismantle his network."

Clayton accepted the envelope, scanning the contents briefly before seeming satisfied. "This will do nicely." He tucked the papers inside his jacket. "I'll ensure these find their way to the appropriate prosecutors and investigators—and I'll make doubly sure Silva doesn't have a chance to come after you to retrieve these anonymously obtained documents." He winked.

Nina frowned. "How can you do that?"

Clayton laughed. "Best you don't know, ma'am."

Relief loosened the last of the knots in Cooper's chest. With these records and Clayton's protection, Darren's organization would be razed.

"I know resources were leveraged to make this possible," added Clayton, his expression turning solemn. "Certain favors might be requested in return someday."

Cooper nodded grimly. He had expected nothing less when requesting assistance going up against someone like Darren. They might have escaped one dangerous entanglement only to land in another, but that was tomorrow's problem.

For now, it was enough to retreat into the warmth and light of the ranch, Nina's hand clasped in his, while Darren's empire crumbled to ashes. Nina and his son were safe, and that was what mattered most.

Chapter 10

MORNING SUNLIGHT FILTERING through lace curtains stirred Nina awake. She smiled drowsily, stretching beneath the covers. The past weeks had passed in a comforting blur of new routines—cooking, milking, cleaning, and gardening. Mundane tasks that now seemed luxuries after so much turmoil. Eventually, she might return to a nine-to-five job, but after her last experience, she was content to take care of Caleb, Cooper, and Mike for the time being.

Slipping from the warm nest of blankets, she followed the rich scent of sizzling bacon toward the kitchen. Pausing unseen in the doorway, her heart swelled at the scene before her.

Cooper stood at the stove, spatula in hand. At his side, Caleb perched on a small step stool, face scrunched in concentration as he carefully turned strips of bacon under his father's watchful eye. Their tousled dark heads were bent together, two sets of intense eyes, the same shape though different colors, focused on their cooking task.

Nina's throat tightened with emotion. How often had she prayed her son would one day know his father's love and protection? That wish was now miraculously reality. She etched each precious detail into her mind to hold close forever.

Sensing her presence, Cooper glanced up, his customary stern expression softening. "Grab a plate. Chef Caleb's almost done here."

"It smells incredible, you two." Nina dropped a kiss on Caleb's head, ruffling his wild curls. Before sitting, she paused to appreciate the cozy domesticity of the scene, so different from the brooding silence that filled the ranch before. Their family was finally whole.

Over breakfast, Nina basked in the easy rhythm between father and son—their bantering jokes and the way Caleb's small face glowed under his father's praise at helping cook warming her. Each ordinary moment now seemed an exquisite gift after so many years starved of affection.

She treasured these stolen moments of normalcy. No dark specter loomed over their shoulders now with Darren gone. They had time to learn each other, to make up for years lost. Time she never thought they'd have again after those first desperate nights arriving on Cooper's doorstep so long ago.

After eating and clearing up, Caleb scampered off to play with Lex and Scooter while Cooper drew Nina outside to the back porch. His brow was furrowed, shoulders tense beneath his flannel shirt.

"I know everything between us started as necessity," he said gruffly. "We didn't choose a reunion. You came to me because you had no choice."

Nina's throat constricted, sensing what was coming. Her pulse stuttered.

Cooper shifted on his feet, voice going low. "With Darren gone, I understand you have choices again. If you wanted to take Caleb and…and make a new life somewhere, I would understand—"

The words pierced Nina's heart. "Is that what you want?" She cut him off more sharply than intended, irrationally hurt.

Cooper looked stunned by the question. He pulled one hand from his pocket, revealing a small velvet box cupped in his broad palm. "I want you to stay. Both of you. Always." Gracefully he dropped to one knee before her on the weathered boards. "If you'll have me."

The vulnerability in his face made Nina's breath catch. With trembling fingers, she opened the box to reveal a modest but beautiful diamond ring nestled inside.

"Yes," she whispered through joyful tears. "Of course, yes."

Strong arms engulfed her then, lifting her off her feet. Through the blur of happy tears, Nina glimpsed Caleb and Mike's faces pressed to the kitchen window, beaming brilliantly. A new chapter was unfolding, but this time they had chosen it together.

ON THE DAY OF THE CEREMONY weeks later, wildflowers swayed gently in the breeze as they got married in the back yard of the ranch. Aside from the officiant, their only guests were Kinsey and the brotherhood, along with Caleb proudly holding the rings on a satin pillow nearly the size of him.

Nina's and Cooper's gazes locked as they said their vows. So much lay uncertain still ahead, but today was a moment of joyful clarity amidst the chaos. They were family now in every sense—husband and wife, father and mother.

As Cooper tenderly kissed her, their friends whooped and cheered loudly. Caleb made exaggerated gagging noises until Cooper playfully scooped him up, kissing his cheek noisily while the boy squealed in delight.

During the casual backyard reception after, lively music filled the air. Nina danced with each of the groomsmen in turn, while Cooper twirled a laughing Kinsey as best he could with her swollen pregnant belly.

Cooper grabbed Nina's hand, pulling her close. "Thank you," he murmured against her hair as they swayed together. Those two words carried a wealth of meaning. *Thank you for our son. For not giving up when I pushed you away. For letting me love you.*

As dusk fell, their little makeshift family raised plastic champagne flutes in a celebratory toast, but suddenly Kinsey gasped aloud, both hands bracing her belly. "Oh. I think the baby's coming."

Chaos erupted as everyone leapt into action. Amidst the flurry of activity getting Kinsey to the hospital, Nina found herself alone with Cooper and Caleb. Her new husband's dumbstruck expression mirrored the amazement swirling inside her. Somehow, despite endless obstacles, they had found their way home.

Later that night, the long-anticipated call came that Kinsey had delivered a healthy baby girl. New life was flourishing even as new dreams took root. The future remained murky in many ways, but Nina faced it now without fear. Their family was woven together by bonds of loyalty and love forged strong when tested.

HOURS LATER, NINA WALKED beside her husband into their bedroom. The backyard wedding had been amazing, and Kinsey's surprise of going into labor had added a dramatic note. Now, it was quiet. Caleb was asleep in his room, and they were in the master bedroom. Their bedroom. Hers, with her husband's.

He came up behind her to nuzzle her neck. "Penny for your thoughts?"

"Just thinking how lucky I am to have you in my life. To have Caleb. To have this second chance. I thought I'd lost you forever." She turned in his arms to face him.

"You almost did, but I'm here now. I'm not going anywhere. I'm yours, Nina. Forever." He kissed her deeply, and she melted into his embrace.

"I love you, Cooper."

"I love you too, baby. More than you'll ever know." He led her to the bed, where he turned her around to start undoing the myriad tiny buttons on the back of her wedding dress. "Damned things," he muttered.

She laughed. "I guess it's true what they say—brides are supposed to look beautiful, but the dresses are a pain in the ass."

"I think you're beautiful, and this dress is definitely a pain in the ass." He chuckled as he worked on the last button.

She stepped out of the dress and stood before him in her white lace bra and panties. "Better?"

He grinned, running his hands over her curves. "Much better."

He unclasped her bra, letting it fall to the floor, then hooked his thumbs in the waistband of her white lace panties and tugged them down.

She stood naked before him, and he gazed at her with a mixture of awe and desire. "God, you're gorgeous."

She blushed, feeling a little self-conscious. "Thank you."

He took her hand and led her to the bed, where he sat down, taking a moment to remove his leg before laying back on the pillows.

"Come here, baby. I need you." His voice was low and husky, and it sent a shiver of anticipation down her spine.

She climbed onto the bed, straddling his hips, but he tapped his chin. "Uh uh. Right here first. Come to me."

She crawled up his body, and he guided her to sit on his face. Her slit hovered above his mouth, and he inhaled deeply, breathing in her scent.

"Mmm, you smell so good. I can't wait to taste you." He pulled her down, and she gasped as his tongue flicked over her clit. The headboard rattled as she clung to it, and he'd barely even begun.

His tongue explored her folds, licking and sucking, and she moaned as he found her most sensitive spots. He lapped at her juices, drinking them in as if they were the sweetest nectar. Her hips rocked against him, and she gasped as he plunged his tongue deep inside her.

"Oh, Cooper, please don't stop." She gripped the headboard tighter, grinding against his mouth as he devoured her.

He groaned, the vibration adding to the sensations, and she cried out as he sucked her clit into his mouth. The pleasure was overwhelming, and her body trembled as he drove her closer to the edge.

"Cooper, I'm so close. Please, I need to come," she begged, needing the release that was just out of reach.

He increased his pace, lapping at her clit and plunging his tongue in and out of her as she writhed above him. The pressure built, and she teetered on the brink of ecstasy.

"Come for me, baby. I want to feel you come on my face." His voice was muffled, but the command was clear.

She let go, surrendering to the waves of pleasure that crashed over her as she came. Her body shook as she cried out, and he held her tightly, prolonging the orgasm until she was spent.

She collapsed against the headboard, panting and gasping for breath. Cooper gently lowered her onto the bed, kissing her tenderly before moving to kneel between her legs. His cock was rock hard when it nudged against her buttocks.

"Do you mind if I take you like this?" He put his hands over hers on the headboard. "I know how much you loved this position before, and I haven't done it in a while, but I think I can manage."

"Of course. I trust you." She smiled, spreading her legs wider and arching her butt backward toward him so he could claim her from behind.

He positioned himself at her entrance, then slowly pushed into her slick heat. She gasped as he stretched her, filling her completely.

"Are you okay?" He asked, pausing to give her time to adjust to his size, which had always been impressive.

"Yes, I'm fine. You feel so good." She moaned, rocking her hips back to take him deeper.

He began to move, thrusting in and out of her with slow, deliberate strokes. The angle allowed him to hit her G-spot, and she cried out as the pleasure intensified.

She gripped the headboard, meeting his thrusts as he picked up the pace. The sound of their bodies connecting echoed through the room, and the bed creaked in protest.

"Nina, I'm close. I need you to come with me." His voice was strained, and she could tell he was holding back.

She reached down between her legs, rubbing her clit as he pounded into her. The pressure built, and she cried out as another orgasm washed over her in a torrent of sensation.

Cooper groaned, his movements becoming erratic as he chased his own release. With one final thrust, he buried himself to the hilt inside her, coming with a shout.

They collapsed onto the bed, spent and satisfied. He pulled her close, and she nestled against his chest, listening to the steady beat of his heart.

"I love you, Cooper. Thank you for giving me the best day of my life."

"I love you too, Nina. Today was the happiest day of my life, and the first of many more to come." He kissed the top of her head, and they drifted off to sleep, content and secure in each other's arms.

Epilogue

THE FIRST INKLING CAME when Nina woke feeling queasy, her stomach churning and roiling distressingly, a few months after their wedding.

"You okay?" Cooper's gravelly voice was soft with concern as he reached over to rub her back. "You look a little green."

"I'm fine. Just feel off for some reason." Nina slowly sat up, willing her insides to settle. As she sat there taking deep breaths, clues from the past week floated through her foggy mind—the constant fatigue dragging her down, waves of nausea striking at odd times, and her overly sensitive nipples.

Cooper watched her closely, brow furrowed. "Could you be...you know...pregnant?" he asked tentatively.

Nina's head jerked up in surprise. "I don't know, I hadn't thought...maybe?" A nervous thrill went through her at the possibility as she rested a hand on her still-flat stomach.

Cooper was up in an instant, pulling on jeans one-handed while he rummaged through a dresser drawer. He grabbed something and came back to press a pregnancy test into Nina's palm.

"I picked this up in town yesterday just in case. After everything we...well..." He trailed off, looking endearingly awkward.

Nina swallowed hard as she stood up on wobbly legs. The two-minute wait was agonizing, both trying not to get their hopes up too high. Finally, she couldn't stand it any longer. Hands trembling wildly, she turned over the test stick to reveal two bright pink lines.

"Oh my goodness," she whispered, tears springing to her eyes. "I'm pregnant."

"We're having a baby?" Cooper's face lit up, arms coming around her so gently as he pulled her close. He gave a surprised bark of laughter, the joyful sound so rare from him. They clung to each other, laughing and crying together with huge smiles on their faces.

When they finally collected themselves enough to go share the news with an elated Caleb, the three of them hugged and dreamed together of the new adventures ahead. Though the future was uncertain, they were venturing into this next chapter as a family. The sweet secret nestled beneath Nina's heart symbolized the hope blooming brilliantly to life for them all.

About Mia

THANK YOU FOR READING! I hope you enjoyed reading this book as much as I loved writing it!

If so, you might be interested in my reader club, where you'll get notice of new releases, specials, and other great goodies (like FREE books and FREE Chapters of upcoming releases).

As a special thank you, **you'll immediately get my book The Boardroom Connection, for FREE when you sign up.** No strings, you can unsubscribe anytime, and I promise I won't blow up your inbox.

What do you think?

YES – I'm in! I want to know the moment you drop a new release and get my FREE book! [Add Link: https://dl.bookfunnel.com/g14g65dcmd]

No, that's alright. I get enough emails, and I'll keep up with your new releases another way.

Again, I hope you enjoyed this book. You can learn more about my newest releases here: https://bwwmlovestories.com/latest-releases/mia-latest/[1]

1.　　https://l.facebook.com/l.php?u=https%3A%2F%2Fbwwmlovestories.com%2Flatest-

releases%2Fmia-

latest%2F%3Ffbclid%3DIwZXh0bgNhZW0CMTAAAR34HFLR7qBe4ZmBHns_e4d0XgNzeL

puTKitrQtc8gfqYam6Jwke4d05P5M_aem_AXZgxaooVqdkRI8v5k6ceTy7Gin_SGSOwZ0mohU

pkMmzR-Suzibzrob5LkW28qL53CXma0uvn_jG_N2FBJWICaiR&h=AT0CMUeqAaRQCxB-

vibJCLOB3BJo5qSFoE64VilifGretJ6ZtzkQOn3BhZ4e4cTX1Dpuw0RpYrElXkhsQlqHZNi1D

ZdWlWOBOS2jn6YcuV5YinE0EhazJOy56rM3zQC4ziRiIOHCHTe8ohj45g&__tn__=-UK-

R&c%5b0%5d=AT06pfvEYO5wdSYGkilnE_RlU_XJQ3YtaKVXM3kw2RVJU7AEHMWZrK

bz4ZVZ5KpHSvCa7Rpb3D9k4_NQuxDiliwHZHAVAvzrcdwCUjfoVuAu6L2M3OoNNZ9qa

And if you get a chance to drop a review or rating, I'd really appreciate it.

Best,

Mia

849xyadSBygYxrAoFCijWjBix80lUGrim2l7h4DWuGnd8vRM3D-hcJAbp-sg41WLy5X32P7Q

About Mylia

IF YOU WOULD LIKE TO be the first to hear about new releases, please join my mailing list[1] and receive a free book. I love to hear from readers, so please feel free to email me at authormashton@yahoo.com.

www.ingramcontent.com/pod-product-compliance
Lightning Source LLC
Chambersburg PA
CBHW061622130726
47996CB00003B/1090